PAPA'S APPLE TREE FARM

Yvonne E. Scott

To order additional copies of this book, contact:
Xlibris
1-888-795-4274
www.Xlibris.com
Orders@Xlibris.com

Library of Congress Control Number: TXu002165571 series of 2019

ISBN: Softcover 978-1-7960-6552-7
EBook 978-1-7960-6551-0

Print information available on the last page

Rev. date: 12/03/2019

Papa's Apple Tree Farm

YVONNE E. SCOTT

In loving memory of my parents the late
Rev. & Mrs. Willie E. Johnson, Sr.

Once upon a time there was a pretty little girl named Chloe. She wanted to go to her Papa's apple tree farm. When they left for Papa's farm, she said, "bye" to her parents.

She was happy to travel with Papa in his five-seated aircraft to the hundred-acre farm where she would see acres of apple trees, tamed animals, and some wild animals too.

Chloe reminisced about Papa's apple tree farm. She remembered previous visits to her grandparents home and could almost smell the fragrance of apples. She thought long and hard about the beautiful apple trees and delicious apples. She thought about the apple's round shape and how firm the apple felt in her hands. She thought about the loud crunching sound that could be heard while biting into an apple. Apples were her favorite fruit to eat.

Soon they arrived at the farm. There was a furry magenta cat waiting to greet them. It was a mother cat and four kittens followed her. "One, two, three, four kittens," counted Chloe. The father cat had a furry cyan coat. The cats went prancing across the farm. Chloe could hear the kittens purr as they approached the back porch.

Suddenly, a purple duck with an orange beak and green eyes went running across the yard towards the big red barn. Papa and Chloe followed the duck into the barn. The duck immediately sat on an egg waiting for it to hatch. Three other ducklings had already hatched and were walking around inside of the barn. The last egg was brown with tiny lilac speckles and spots. As the egg began to crack, smiles of joy appeared on Chloe's face. At last, the duckling came out of its eggshell and joined the other ducklings. "One, two, three, four ducklings," counted Chloe.

After a while, Chloe wanted to go inside of the dome shaped house to say hi to her grandmother, MiMi. The house set on top of a mountainous hill. When she went inside of the house she looked up to see the skylight in the ceiling. Then a gust of wind blew against a crystal window pane in the kitchen. There were cups of ice cold apple juice on a table near the window. As she looked out of the window, Chloe could see, in the distance, a big kite flying high toward the blue sky.

The yellow sun was shining through the window. Its light made the crystals in the window pane sparkle, which caused everything to look brighter inside and outside of the dome house. The dome house was a very large place to live and had many rooms. Chloe loved visiting her grandparents. When she accidentally found out that her parents might split up, she had hoped to one day live with Papa and MiMi. She prayed that her family would always be together.

Grandmother, MiMi fixed a small snack for everyone: fresh sliced apples. A sweet aroma filled the house, but there was no special treat in sight. “The cake is in the oven and will be ready soon,” said MiMi. “Oh, great!” said Chloe. “In the meantime, I will let the Little Lady see some of the animals,” said Papa. When Papa said little lady, he was referring to Chloe, then he took her outside. “Quack, quack!” said the ducks. They watched the ducks run around the farmyard.

They watched some of the other animals: Chickens, pigs, cows, goats, sheep, and horses. Their beige-furry dog went with them as they rode in the aircraft throughout the farm. They finally went to see acres of apple trees which were filled with green and red apples. At noon, the sun got extremely hot. Papa had gotten exhausted, he had also video taped the farm to let the family watch together later. They went back to the comfortable dome house.

In the afternoon Chloe's parents, uncle, and other friends came to visit the farm. Uncle brought a card and a vase full of fresh flowers as a gift. The vase looked wet, but it was not wet. Chloe did not have x-ray vision, but she could see water inside of the vase. The vase was tall, clear, and shiny. The flowers were magenta apple blossoms. The water inside the vase kept the flowers fresh.

Uncle sat the vase of flowers on the table in front of Chloe and read the card to her. He read, "You are as beautiful as a bouquet of apple blossoms, happy birthday!" The card and flowers were for Chloe's fourth birthday. Everyone said "Happy Birthday, Chloe!"

Later, everyone rode in jeeps to go on a safari into the forest to find wild animals. This part of the property was separated from the farm by the woods, a lake, a huge terrain, and a tall electric fence. They saw a large black and white-striped zebra and a small baby zebra. They saw Chloe's most favorite unique animal, the big tall giraffe eating leaves from a tree in the forest. Also, there were elephants, lions, and tigers roaming through the forest near the apple tree farm.

After the safari ended, everyone went inside the house and washed their hands. MiMi put one, two, three, four candles on the cake. Chloe closed her eyes, made a wish, and blew out all the candles. Everyone sat down at the table together then asked God to bless the food and family. They watched the video and enjoyed dinner with the birthday cake for dessert. They continued to celebrate Chloe's birthday for the entire evening. There were ten gifts with one computer game included just for Chloe at Papa's apple tree farm.

FARM ANIMALS

CAT

CHICKEN

COW

DOG

DUCK

GOAT

HORSE

PIG

SHEEP

SAFARI ANIMALS

ELEPHANT

GIRAFFE

LION

TIGER

ZEBRA

THE ALPHABET LIST

Apple

Bye

Cat

Duck

Egg

Face

Go

Hi

Ice

Juice

Kite

Light

MiMi

No

Oh

PaPa

Quack

Run

Sun

To

Uncle

Vase

Wet

X-ray

You

Zebra

NUMBERS

1 - One

2 - Two

3 - Three

4 - Four

5 - Five

6 - Six

7 - Seven

8 - Eight

9 - Nine

10 - Ten

About the Book

This book is about a preschooler who loves to visit her grandparents. It reveals the value of family and friends. It also contains teacher-friendly text including colors, alphabets, and numbers that children can learn and recognize. Scripture quotations, from the King James Version (KJV) of the Holy Bible are for inspiration to the reader. When looking at this book with children who are learning to read, help them remember pronunciations by saying words slowly. Repeating the word should encourage the children to say the word as well. The colorful words may help children get familiar with the spelling of specific colors. This book also provides an opportunity for children to make a distinction between characters.

About the Author

The author, Yvonne Scott grew up in a family of 12 children. She was employed as a children's nursery assistant during her teenage years. She completed 35 years of service as an employee and completed accredited courses in Philosophy and Religion at Clemson University, Clemson, S.C.; also traveled and completed Study Abroad courses in Turkey and Greece. She has received a Bachelor Degree in Theology from North Carolina College of Theology; served on the Board of Directors of the Oconee County Habitat for Humanity in S.C.; served as President of Seneca River Family Life Institute Improvement Association; served on the Executive Board of the Baptist Educational and Missionary Convention of S.C.; served as the 1st female Moderator of Union# 3 of Seneca River Baptist Association; served on the Trustee Board of Seneca River Baptist Sunday School Congress of Christian Education; and served 18 years as Pastor of St. Mark Baptist Church in Westminster, S.C. Scriptures of inspiration:

Proverbs 22:6 KJV
Train up a child in the way he should go: and when he is old, he will not depart from it.

Romans 10:9 KJV
That if thou shalt confess with thy mouth the Lord Jesus, and shalt believe in thine heart that God hath raised him from the dead, thou shalt be saved.

CPSIA information can be obtained
at www.ICGtesting.com
Printed in the USA
BVHW020941181219
566812BV00017B/28/P